MW00903768

Would you like FREE coloring pages & worksheets for this book? Download them at the address below -

Worksheets for
Bluster Blue Jay

Bluster Blue Jay:
Not MY Fault!

Fearless & Friends

By Mother Melania
Illustrated by Cayce-Marie Halsell

bookconnect.review/dp/worksheetsblusterbluejay

Check out more of Mother Melania's books at
amazon.com/author/mothermelania

bit.ly/Moses-Burning-Bush

*Old Testament Stories
for Children*

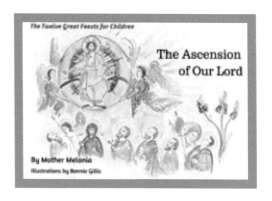

bit.ly/Ascension-Lord

*The Twelve Great
Feasts for Children*

bit.ly/Pascha-Feast

*The Three-Day Pascha: Orthodox
Christian Easter Stories for Children*

bit.ly/Scooter-Gets-Point

*The Adventures of
Kenny & Scooter*

PLEASE NOTE -Links are case sensitive

Bluster Blue Jay:
Not MY Fault!

By Mother Melania

Illustrated by Cayce-Marie Halsell

Fearless the Fire Duck was going camping. He worked hard all year keeping the Duck Pond safe. Finally, he had a chance to relax!

Fearless asked Grateful the Crow to join him. Grateful, who was happy when anyone asked him along, gratefully agreed.

You remember Grateful, don't you? He used to be called Greedy until Charity the Church Mouse taught him a lesson about love and sharing.

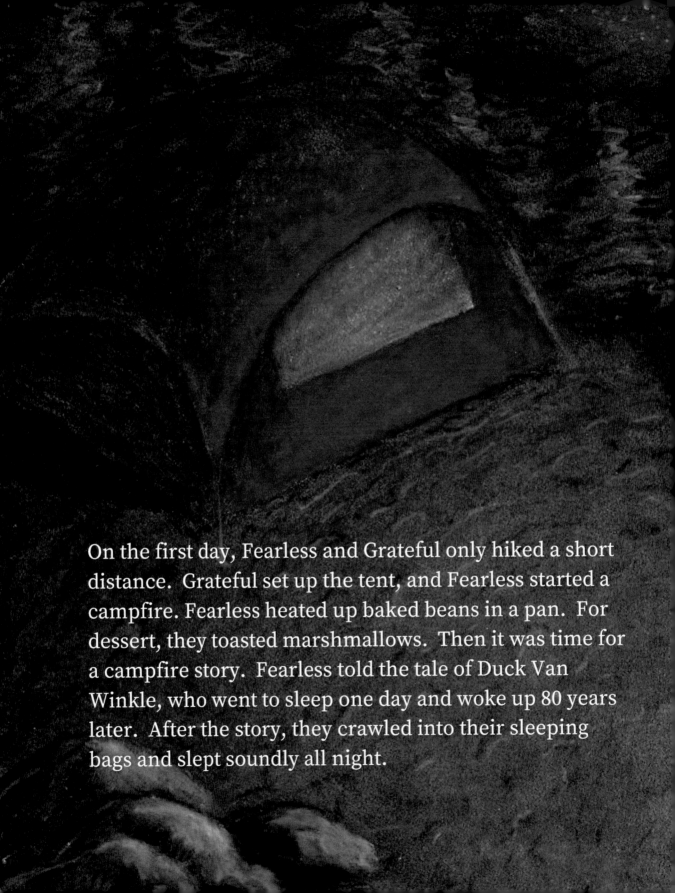

On the first day, Fearless and Grateful only hiked a short distance. Grateful set up the tent, and Fearless started a campfire. Fearless heated up baked beans in a pan. For dessert, they toasted marshmallows. Then it was time for a campfire story. Fearless told the tale of Duck Van Winkle, who went to sleep one day and woke up 80 years later. After the story, they crawled into their sleeping bags and slept soundly all night.

The next morning, they were ready for a long hike. "Where should we go, Fearless?" Grateful asked.

"I haven't hiked up to Lookout Point for a long time. Why don't we try that?" Fearless replied.

"Sounds good to me, Fearless. You lead the way."

They had not gotten far when they came upon Bluster Blue Jay. Bluster was trying to go to Lookout Point, too, but he was lost. Not that he would ADMIT that he was lost. No, he wanted everyone to think he always knew what he was doing.

"Hi, Bluster," said Fearless. "What brings you here?"

"I'm hiking," Bluster replied. "I'm a great hiker, you know. I made it all the way here to Lookout Point in just an hour!"

"Umm, this isn't Lookout Point. We're still miles away from there."

Now Bluster changed his tune. "Well, if I'm not there yet, it must be the fault of my compass. All that silly compass ever does is point north!"

"But Bluster," Grateful replied, "Compasses aren't supposed to tell you where to go. They just tell you where north is, and you have to figure out where you're going from there."

"I know that! I was just trying to make sure that YOU did!" the blue jay blustered.

"Anyway, if you're going to Lookout Point, we can go together. With my marvelous sense of direction, I can help you a lot," Bluster continued.

Fearless and Grateful looked at each other. Bluster wasn't the easiest animal to be around, but he needed help – even though he wouldn't admit it. Fearless gave Grateful a little nod.

Grateful said, "Yes, we ARE going to Lookout Point, and you're welcome to join us."

"Great!" Bluster replied. "You're so lucky to have me with you!" He didn't say, "Thank you." It never occurred to him that his friends were being kind to take him along.

Fearless led the way, with Grateful next, and Bluster trailing along behind. Up and up they climbed. When lunchtime came, Grateful made a little campfire again. Fearless poured the beans into a pan.

"Yuck, baked beans!" Bluster said in a sulky voice. "Nobody likes baked beans."

Fearless took a deep breath. "I do like baked beans, but you're welcome to make whatever you brought."

Bluster, who had not remembered to bring lunch, said grandly, "That's okay, Fearless. I don't want to embarrass you with my great cooking!"

Fearless knew better than to reply. In silence, they all scooped their beans with corn chips. Then, they all toasted marshmallows.

Fearless and Grateful toasted their marshmallows to a beautiful golden brown. Bluster burned his to a crisp.

"Hey!" he yelled. "You gave me a bad marshmallow!"

Fearless sighed.   "Maybe it's time to start hiking again," Grateful said.

So, they continued up the hill. Grateful suggested that Bluster go in the middle. That way, Fearless could lead the way and Grateful could be behind Bluster to make sure that he was okay.

Bluster just ignored Grateful's suggestion and went on ahead. He was sure he was the best hiker there.

Grateful didn't say anything. He was too busy trying to BE grateful. "I'm grateful that Fearless is here. I'm grateful that we were able to help Bluster. I'm grateful that Charity was kind to me when I was greedy. I want to keep being grateful."

Meanwhile, the climbing was becoming harder and harder. Bluster was breathing in little puffs. He was having a really hard time.

"Bluster, are you okay?" Fearless asked kindly. "May I help you?"

Glancing back at Fearless, Bluster said, "I don't need any help. I'm a GREAT hik..."

Unfortunately, Bluster WASN'T a great hiker. He had forgotten a very important rule – always watch where you're going. So he missed his step and went tumbling back down the path onto Fearless. Then the two of them rolled onto Grateful.

Fearless and Grateful each had injured wings and legs, but Bluster was just fine. Now it was Fearless and Grateful who needed help.

"Bluster, you need to go get Polly the Paramedic Parrot," Fearless said calmly. "We can't fly, and we can't walk."

For the first time in a long time, Bluster stopped blustering.

Fearless made Bluster repeat the directions over and over. Finally, he was ready to go. On the long trip back down the mountain, Bluster had lots of time to think. He began to see how kind his friends had been and how badly he had acted. When he returned with Polly, he was a different bird.

"You can't be! We already have a Grateful!" chuckled Fearless.

"Well, then, just call me Grateful Two!"

Bluster Blue Jay: Not MY Fault!

from *Fearless and Friends*

Story © copyright 2010 by Mother Melania
Illustrations © copyright 2010 by Cayce-Marie Halsell

All rights reserved.

Published by Holy Assumption Monastery
1519 Washington St.
Calistoga, CA 94515

Phone: (707) 942-6244
Website: https://holyassumptionmonastery.com
Email: sisters@holyassumptionmonastery.com

If you liked this book, please consider
purchasing the other books in the series

bit.ly/Capers-Harry

bit.ly/Greedy-Crow

bit.ly/Mimi-Mynah

And please check out our monastery's line of journals at
amazon.com/author/holyassumptionmonastery

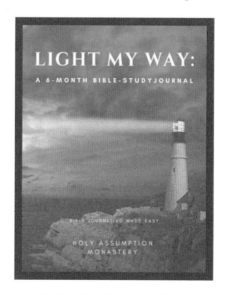

bit.ly/Every-Thanks

bit.ly/Light-My-Way

PLEASE NOTE -Links are case sensitive

Please leave a review of this book on Amazon—

bit.ly/Review-Bluster-Blue-Jay

We're always looking for feedback and ways to improve!

Thanks so much, and God bless you!

ABOUT THE AUTHOR AND ILLUSTRATOR

Mother Melania is the abbess of Holy Assumption Monastery in Calistoga, California. She has enjoyed working with children all of her life. In addition to The Three-Day Pascha series, she has written several other series of children's books, focusing on Scriptural stories and Great Feasts of the Church, and celebrating the virtues.

Cayce-Marie Halsell is an Orthodox Christian iconographer and illustrator. She lives in Santa Barbara, California with her family. You can see more of her work at www.cmhicons.weebly.com